To Natalie,

The Music Maker of my life…

www.mascotbooks.com

Melody's Gift

©2019 Corbett Babb. All Rights Reserved. No part of this publication may be reproduced, stored in a retrieval system or transmitted in any form by any means electronic, mechanical, or photocopying, recording or otherwise without the permission of the author.

For more information, please contact:
Mascot Books
620 Herndon Parkway, Suite 320
Herndon, VA 20170
info@mascotbooks.com

Library of Congress Control Number: 2018910920

CPSIA Code: PRT0119A
ISBN-13:978-1-68401-606-8

Printed in the United States

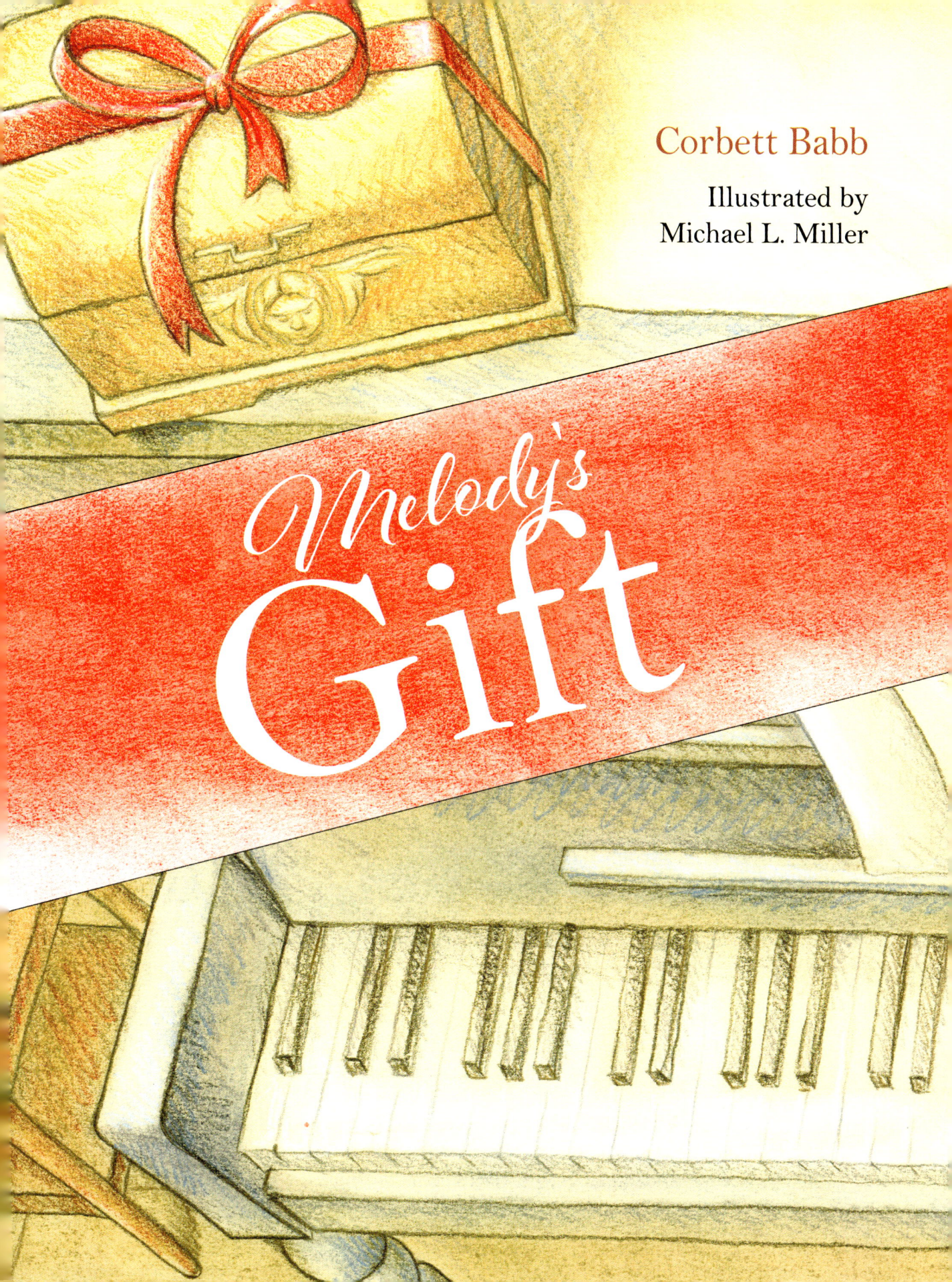

Tucked away in the back of the antique store, the old, discarded jewelry box named Melody sighed a long, sorrowful sigh and nodded off to sleep. She dreamed of the treasures she once held so close, only to awaken, as she always did, covered by a cold blanket of dust and nothing but darkness within.

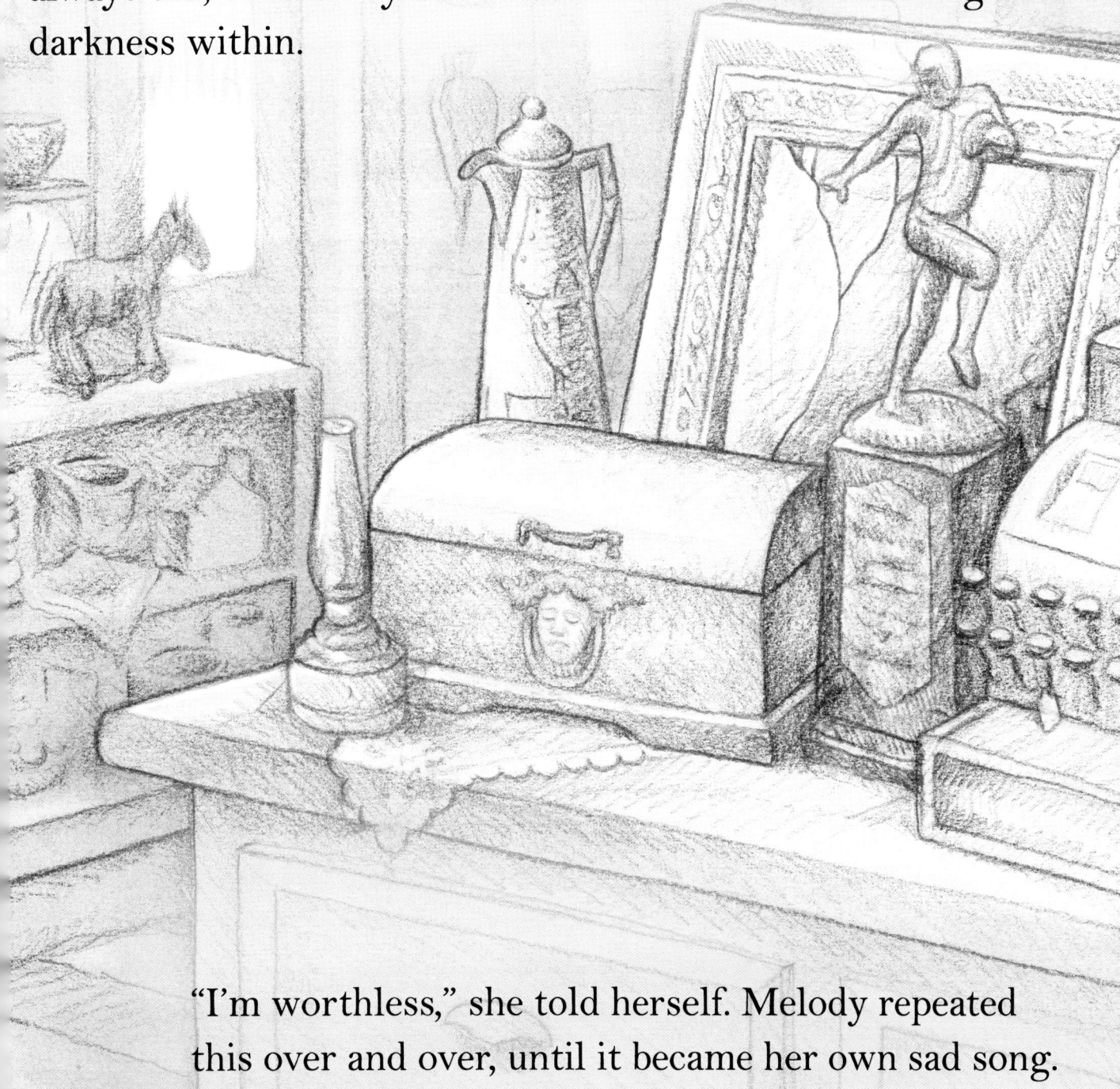

"I'm worthless," she told herself. Melody repeated this over and over, until it became her own sad song.

It hadn't always been this way. She once lived in a house filled with laughter and love. Her blue, velvet insides held many treasures, like earrings, bracelets, rings, and precious stones. Her hinges worked freely, and she sang a sweet song each time she was opened.

But that was long ago. Her rusty hinges ached at the thought. Her scratches and scars grew deeper, reaching their way to her emptiness inside. She stood lost among the other once valuables. Quiet, forgotten…sad.

Is there any use for a jewelry box who can't sing anymore? she thought.

The floorboards of the antique shop creaked as The Listener strode through the door. His purposeful steps woke Melody from her usual slumber. The Listener paused for a moment as he scanned the old, dust-covered wares in front of him. He closed his eyes and drew his head high.

What is he doing? she thought.

Melody wished she could slide herself along the table just an inch so she could see him better, but an old cash register blocked her way. A cracked mirror reflected her faded surface.

The Listener did what he always did when searching for something special. He prayed. He thought. He listened…

Suddenly, his eyes opened and The Listener resumed his determined steps in Melody's direction. It had been a long time since anyone had walked toward her. She gasped as the music wheel within her turned *ever... so... slightly.*

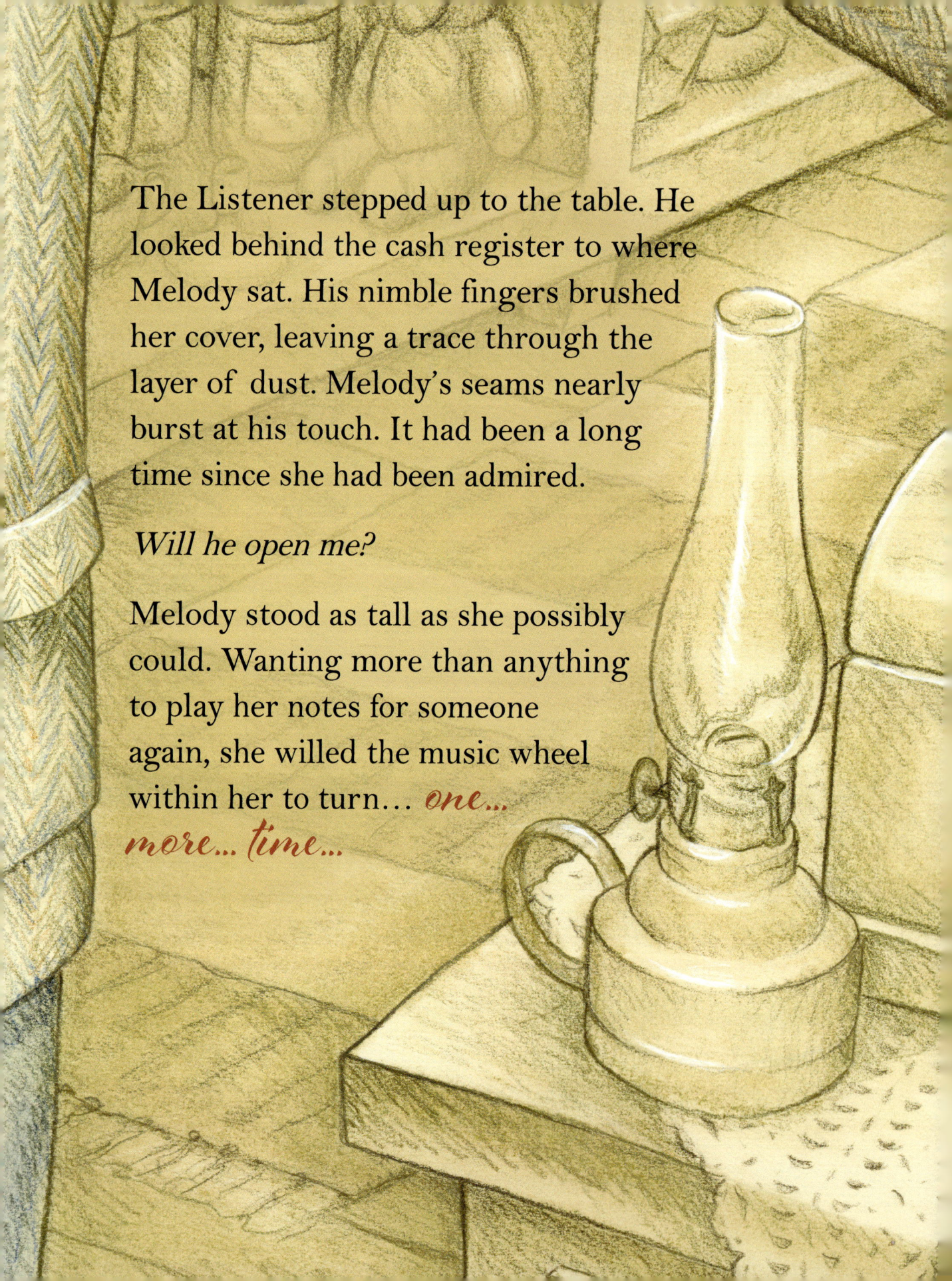

The Listener stepped up to the table. He looked behind the cash register to where Melody sat. His nimble fingers brushed her cover, leaving a trace through the layer of dust. Melody's seams nearly burst at his touch. It had been a long time since she had been admired.

Will he open me?

Melody stood as tall as she possibly could. Wanting more than anything to play her notes for someone again, she willed the music wheel within her to turn… *one… more… time…*

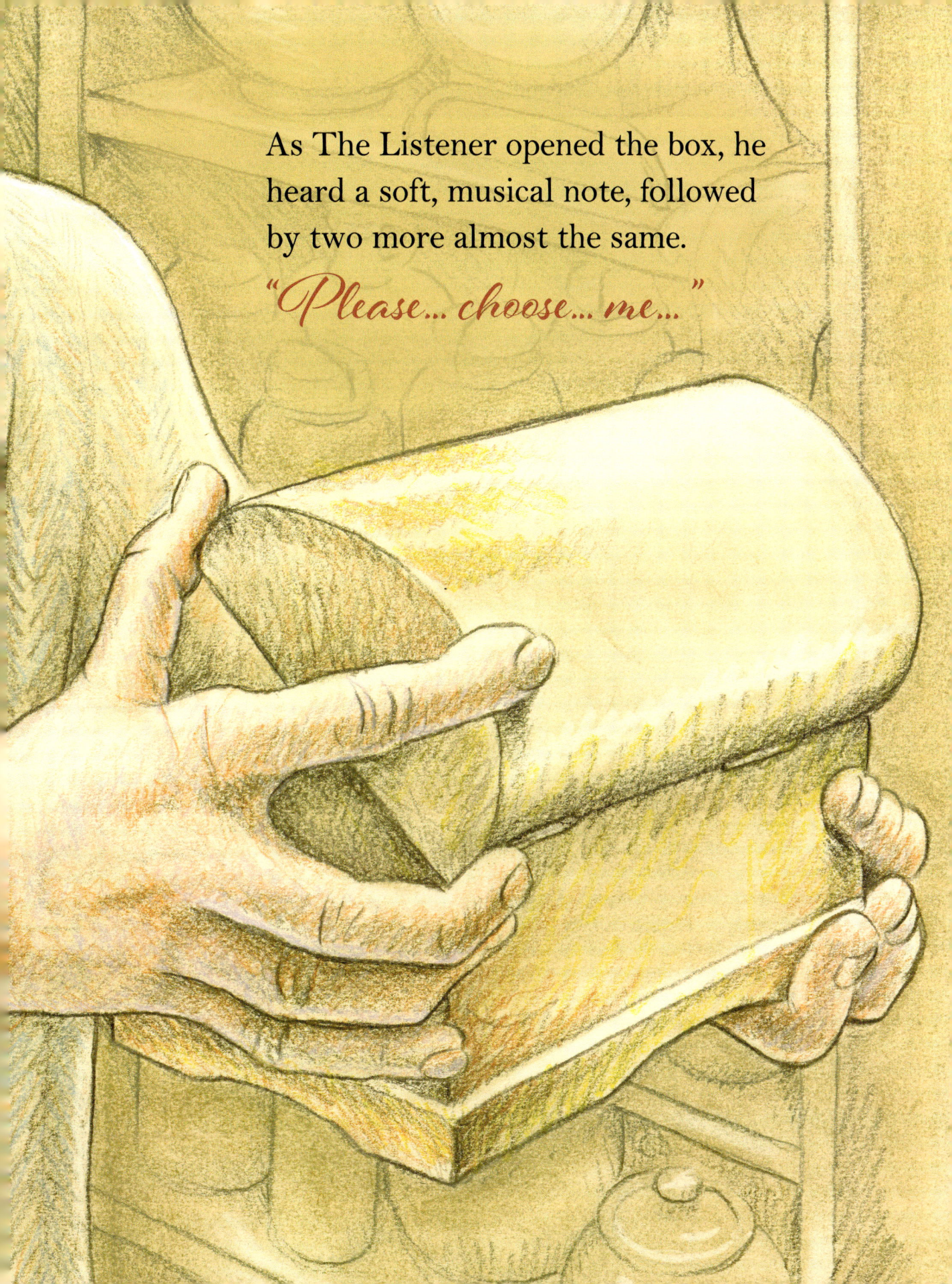

As The Listener opened the box, he heard a soft, musical note, followed by two more almost the same.

"Please... choose... me..."

The Listener brushed his fingers over Melody's soft, blue velvet, and smiled quietly to himself. Closing the lid, he studied the places on her surface where other hands had worn through the varnish. Opening the lid again, four more soft notes floated through the quiet of the room, followed by one more, barely heard…

"I… will… love… her……………too."

He had found his gift for the Music Maker.

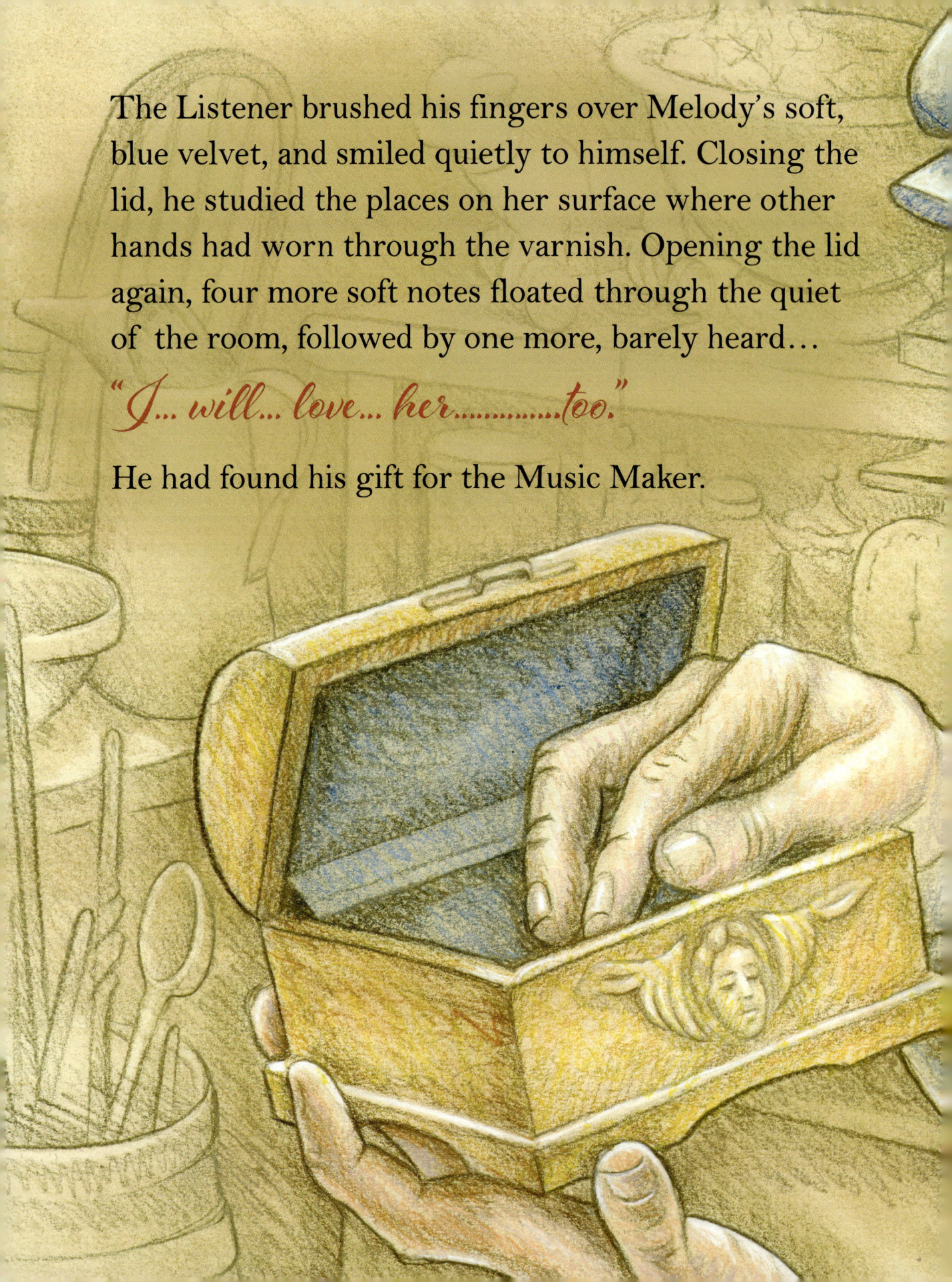

The Listener tied a red ribbon around Melody and placed her on the Music Maker's piano. In this new place, Melody trembled. The light made her notice all the scratches on her outside. Peering over the edge of the piano, she imagined herself falling to the wooden floor below.

Suddenly, Melody felt something warm and familiar flood over her. The notes started slow, but eventually they wove themselves together.

Music.

These weren't the same sounds she used to make over and over when small hands opened her. This time, small hands made their own songs.

Melody shied away from the light as her lid opened. Her only song was the creaking of her old hinges.

The Music Maker pulled three shiny bracelets from her wrists and placed them inside. Pulling back her long, blond curls, she remembered the rings on her fingers and slid them off as well before placing them on the blue velvet. Melody planted her feet firmly to the top of the piano and sang six bold notes for all to hear.

Maybe, I am good for something!

The Listener gently patted the Music Maker on the head as he eased past her. Her hands began to glide across the piano keys faster, striking notes that caused Melody to hold tight.

Before long, the Music Maker began to sing. Her sweet voice matched the ebb and flow of the piano notes as Melody held new treasures and swayed to the rhythm of it all…

As the Music Maker made music, The Listener closed his eyes and listened, and Melody lived and loved once again.

About the Author

Dr. Corbett Babb is a husband, father of three sons, and a middle school principal. He has been an educator for 25 years, and in 2016, was recognized by the National Institute of School Leadership as a Pennsylvania Distinguished Principal.

About the Illustrator

Michael Miller is an art educator in the Wyomissing Area School District, where he has taught both elementary and high school students for the past 20 years. He has also coordinated numerous collaborative public art projects in the Greater Reading area. *Melody's Gift* is the third children's book he has illustrated.